Homography

Biography

Nathan Evans is a writer and performer based in London. Publishers of his poetry include Magma, Fourteen Poems, Broken Sleep, Muswell Press, Royal Society of Literature, Poetry Wales and Manchester Metropolitan University; his debut collection *Threads* was longlisted for Polari First Book Prize 2017; his second collection *CNUT* is published by Inkandescent. His debut novella *One Last Song* was an iNewspaper 'best book' for Pride and longlisted for Polari Book Prize 2024; his collection of short fiction *All the Young Queers* is published by Inkandescent; he is a recipient of an Arts Council Developing Your Creative Practice grant.

Nathan's work in theatre and film has been toured by the British Council, archived in the British Film Institute, broadcast on Channel 4 and presented at venues including Royal Festival Hall and Royal Vauxhall Tavern. He hosts BOLD Queer Poetry Soirée and has done events for National Poetry Library, Charleston Small Wonder Festival, Stoke Newington Literary Festival, Hastings Book Festival and Rye Arts Festival; he teaches on the BA Creative Writing and English Literature at London Metropolitan University and is editor at Inkandescent.

www.nathanevans.co.uk

Praise for *CNUT*

*'A kaleidoscopic journey through shifting landscapes brimming with
vivid imagery, playfulness and warmth.'*
KEITH JARRETT

*'Evans's poetry addresses vital issues of our time
with biting wit, seething passion and electrifying skill.'*
MATTHEW TODD

*'A universal backyard collection of the urban/urbane reimagined, of the
domestic/fantastic retold,
of the ravishingly re-readable.'*
GERRY POTTER

'Poignant, humane and uncompromising'
STEPHEN MORRISON-BURKE

Praise for *Threads*

*'In this bright and beautiful collaboration, poetry and photography join
hands, creating sharp new ways
to picture our lives and loves.'*
NEIL BARTLETT

*'A poetic, performative landscape where the everyday bumps up against
memories, dreams and magic.'*
MARISA CARNESKY

*'A winning blend of words and images, woven together
with passion and wit.'*
PAUL BURSTON

Praise for *One Last Song*

'An enchanting romance—funny, touching and inspiring'
STEPHEN FRY

'It's very funny, very touching and has the absolute ring of truth about
it. One can't but fall in love with these two more or less impossible
people as they fall in love with each other.'
SIMON CALLOW

'Touching. Heartwarming. Funny. Sad.
Adored this book and couldn't put it down.'
JONATHAN HARVEY

'A necessary love story, both profoundly moving and profoundly
optimistic. It will inevitably infiltrate your heart.'
MARTIN SHERMAN

'When we forget our queer elders who lived so we could fly, we forget
ourselves; Nathan Evans has painted them with humour, love, truth
and glory. This is a gem of a novella.'
ADAM ZMITH

'A beautiful, smouldering, hilarious and sparkling testament to queer
intimacy and the revolutionary potency of queer creative activism.
Every page filled my heart with Pride.'
DAN GLASS

Praise for *All the Young Queers*
'original, compelling and cleverly crafted'
JON RANSOM

'An astonishingly accomplished range of stories, beautifully written. I
laughed, I cried, I nodded my head in recognition.'
IQBAL HUSSAIN

Inkandescent

First published by Inkandescent, 2025
Text Copyright © 2025 Nathan Evans
Cover Design Copyright © 2025 Michael Long
Author Photograph Copyright © 2025 Justin David

EU GPSR Authorised Representative
LOGOS EUROPE, 9 rue Nicolas Poussin, 17000, LA ROCHELLE, France
E-mail: Contact@logoseurope.eu

A CIP catalogue record for this book
is available from the British Library

Printed and bound by Ashford Colour Ltd, Gosport, Hants PO13 0FW

ISBN 978-1-912620-38-8 (paperback)
ISBN 978-1-912620-39-5 (Kindle e-book)

1 3 5 7 9 10 8 6 4 2

www.inkandescent.co.uk

for Sarah
& for all my sisters

Also by Nathan Evans

Poetry
Threads
CNUT

Fiction
One Last Song
All the Young Queers

Homography

Nathan Evans

Contents

Foreword

As the world tightens, and the banks take down their rainbow flags, we need books like this.

Homography chronicles gay male experience—the long journey from a shared inheritance of shame to a sense of arrival, a completion. Our common queer heritage is remembered and elevated, a church within itself. It is vital that we write our own narratives, that we avoid becoming the story of the story. To paraphrase Adrienne Rich, this book is not 'the story of the wreck, but the wreck itself'.

These are poems of belonging, songs to courage, to radical hope. Through delicate and careful imaginings, Evans suggests how we are all built from one another—an arm from one man, the eye of another. How we take resilience from one, and euphoria from another. In doing so, we create a metaphor for us all during this uncertain moment in history—that we are of one another, indivisible, a strange unity.

We need each other in times like these. We need these poems.

Joelle Taylor, May 2025

Introduction

I write this in a week when London Gay Symphony Orchestra—with whom I've played for almost thirty years—have performed the *Symphonic Dances from West Side Story*; the music for the show from which this piece is adapted was written by Leonard Bernstein (1918-1990) with lyrics by Stephen Sondheim (1930-2021), both of whom were gay men, and it's not difficult to read the song 'Somewhere' as an expression of hope that 'someday' we'll 'find' a 'time' and 'place' of tolerance for *all* of 'us'. I found it incredibly moving to be part of that particular performance, with that particular group of musicians—from all branches of our LGBTQ+ family tree—because it feels as if, just as we've finally found somewhere like that place, and begun to build a home in it, the foundations are being torn up, brick by brick.

This is also the week in which the UK Supreme Court have ruled that the terms 'woman' and 'sex' in the Equality Act refer only to a biological woman and to biological sex—a decision that has far-reaching ramifications for trans women and men, restricting access to services, spaces—and places.

This is also the year when Trump has returned to power in the United States Of America—home of Bernstein and Sondheim—and the shock waves of that are being felt across the planet, not least in his attack on diversity, equity and inclusion.

Of course, in many countries throughout the world, our rights are not recognised, or are actively supressed; in some countries, they still kill us. Here in the United Kingdom, LGBT rights are a relatively recent development: homosexuality wasn't legalised until 1967; I was born in 1974, so progress has happened mostly in my lifetime. When I was a child, homophobic bullying was on the curriculum in every playground; when I was a teenager, it was sanctioned by government legislation. When I became a 'practising homosexual', I became a criminal: I had turned nineteen but the age of consent remained twenty-one. I wasn't of the generation picked off by pandemic; I was the generation who grew up under the shadow of it, one which has only slowly lifted with societal and medical advancements.

The bad stuff doesn't just disappear now things are better, and that's something I unpack in these poems: many of us have travelled a long, winding (and yellow-brick) road before we've felt at 'home' in our own skins. There have been gatekeepers—little green men in our heads who parrot the stories we've been told about ourselves—and there have been detours into poppy fields—when you've been schooled in self-hatred, it can require a bit of 'extra-curricular' to be able to love others. But lovers there have been, and we've found friends (of Dorothy), chosen families, 'melted' enemies—outside ourselves and in. The ending hasn't always been a happy one, but sometimes we've made peace with the places we've come from. Often with a little help from (ruby slippers and) fairy godfathers.

This collection also celebrates our queer ancestors—those bold pioneers who fought for the freedoms we currently enjoy. It

14

celebrates our queer spaces—some no longer here, some in present danger—places where we can be together, in physical not digital form. And it celebrates our queer (sub) cultures—there may be references you do not understand, so I've written some hopefully helpful notes, at the end.

I write from my own experience: I cannot represent the experiences of all our LGBTQIA family, but I can use forms as diverse as our community. Sometimes a poem has chosen 'normativity', to rhyme and stanza conventionally; sometimes a poem has wanted to play, to do things its own way.

And that's exactly as it should be, and always has been, and always will be. The world can seem a pretty hopeless place, at the moment, and it has felt so before; I hope this collection can give some hope for our collective queer future.

Nathan Evans, April 2025

Bold

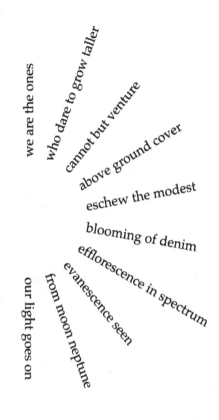

we are the ones

who dare to grow taller

cannot but venture

above ground cover

eschew the modest

blooming of denim

efflorescence in spectrum

evanescence seen

from moon neptune

our light goes on

travelling

Blitz Club & Caravan

we who never felt at home
at home followed hazard-tape
roads to a green-for-go city
where we could finally belong
in our own bodies

       made-up & magpied
       we rode underground
       carriages to Trash Palaces
       Substations & Ghettos
       of our generation

camped hours in star-crossed
gutters to darken doorways descend
stairways to havens where flowers
not yet in bloom walled rooms
we wanted to live in

       learning to dance on our own
       two feet glitching the beat
       like dirty CDs until third pint
       streamed pelvis intervened
       & we murdered floors

in lightshows singing rainbows
not bluetones our every limb
scrolling & tapping
into pheromones sweating
from ancestral ceilings

we were Blitz Club & Caravan
Dionysian Apollonian
hunting cigarette smoke
undergrowth for hyacinths
& gathering them

in form unexpected unfiltered
sculptural not digital
our phones for exchanged numbers
not Ubers we Oystered
uncapitalised zones

to first homes shared
with chosen sisters brothers
others our seconds always there
Marvellous Mother Misfit
until they were not

& now we are permitted
a place at the table to order
from the same menu to have
any petaled-peccadillo beamed
to our own bedroom

while only memories mirrorball
luxury flats Crossrail tracks
as the city instars again
& the young heel their own
way as Dorothy as we

Scar Tissue (Mansize)

(i)   He began to grow breasts, age almost thirteen. *That's how they start,* his mother lowered her voice and his t-shirt; in her disapproval of this development, there could be no doubt.

(ii)   Forking fingers through the boy's soft soil, a doctor declared the tubers *normal:* seasons turn; gardens get turned; clods get broken.

(iii) This timeline was too free-reign for the mother's liking: her father had drilled the hard lines a man must be grown in; any ambiguities were best weeded swiftly from her son.

(iv) He would see fourteen soon, stay a fortnight from the classroom. Classmates should be given no reason—his shame silenced, interred as a womb's afterword.

(v)   The interrogation was excruciating, extenuating; confirmation climbed blackboards, rooted in playing fields—the boy was *so* gay he was all but a girl.

(vi) Awaking from amputation, he found aureoles glaring up at him, anger arching each of them; these, he knew, should stay straightjacketed in Games changing rooms.

(vii) Amid anaesthetic dregs, he read redemption and—making his bed a makeshift desk—he pledged this homework must be his best, his mum made proud yet.

(viii)It had been set for Biology, by the same 'Sir' who taught Religious Studies—his lesson to pent pubescents, the holiness of the human reproductive system.

(ix) The boy's petrol patterns sirened nurses from stations, wrecked them on crude slogans: it was 1987, his inscriptions inspired by TV tombstones, tabloid typesettings.

(x) *Don't die of ignorance! Don't bend for a friend!* And to demons, between lines: *Come out and do not enter me again!*

(xi) How many flocking Florences had nursed their own dead, were nursing their own death? How could a school have given commendation to such casual sexual condemnation?

(xii) Boy grew to man, demons still in him; his nipples now thrill him, but he can't help wondering how he might be growing had the girl not been dug from him.

Uphill Farming

let the combine harvester of capitalism cum
  coz we're shit-shovelling to freedom, hun!

don't fly no more but fucking bareback
  is boarding with a litre of elixir rucksacked

& however deep we plough each other's asses
  we'll not seed babies, immunodeficiencies

only butterflies beat these gurls' guts! but ear
  earth's solar plexus—& hear that?—our ideas

jet the planet—non-linear, systematic—
  yield models, non-hierarchical & holistic

which rise—spiralised, honeyed as hives—
  sweet harvest of protest—see!—queer lives

cut free from family trees flourish, destinies
  rerouted into husbandry of diversities!

An Accidental Arborist

How many men had Sir laid
seed in & its potentialities
had liquified in cavities
like caterpillars unbutterflied?

How many a spit pit
had bedded in brains
& unbeknown become trim
bonsai or towering brute?

How many saviours
& dictators could yield
from identical raw material
in a single man's desires?

Old Queen as Ecosystem

I grew up
between hard heart and rock
of family and school   law and bible
each root downed   nourishment found
was stake upon an even ground
each florid frond a win over winds
changing tune in lento tempo to relative major
now old but bold   bent but unbowed
I have made myself home
to multiple organisms   Boys buzz blossoms
palating first pollen   Fetishists feather-up
in leafy locker rooms   Twinks sing old-favourites
over new-fangled twig percussion   Polyamorists branch out
Jocks bough up   Monogamists nest in nooks   Otters strip
bark to build designer dens with Geek boyfriends   Pups lick
sap and low-hanging Daddies toss rewards to them
Bears winter
in my trunk's
hollow centre
spooned around
Cubs and Chasers
Pigs rut roots for musky delicacies
Queers party in underground arches   Discreets bury histories
Trans migrate microclimates   are one
with all of us

Bulbs

locked

long months

in deep discrete dark

we take as present this present

absorbing   grounding   transforming

as light lengthens   then rising   realising

we have not weathered this alone

we are spectrum

Colour Wash

- mix two parts powder to one of water
- apply, let dry, then sand until level
- if only my cracks were as easy to fill
- with one coat, two, I could paint over
- you

calling me by your names.

turning down my hand in taglines.

shaming my sassing in the dressing-up competition.

ribbing my ribboning limbs as I run the egg-and-spoon.

passing on passing me the ball.

saying I sound *like a girl*.

making me *a man about it*.

goading me to give *good as you get*.

crucifying me on fingers in every school corridor.

backsiding into corners in each classroom I enter.

wigging me a woman in the end-of-term production.

equating feminisation with humiliation.

gagging when they *ram it down* your television.

auguring expulsion if I *take that turn*.

styling out such lives as *chosen*.

knowing *someone* but not acknowledging I'm one.

phrasing it off as *a phase*.

telltale-ing on my *tendencies*.

morsing messages then making out I mixed them.

critiquing my vowels' curlicues whenever I call home.

professing it's *not a problem*.

doubting I must *give it mention*.

taking the life of our friendship.

burying my breaks niche deep.

serving notice of my infamy like a death in the family.

evaluating and not valuing me.

Red

& yellow

& pink

& green

purple &

orange &

blue

we can sing rainbows over corporate logos

Christmas commercials

reality TV shows

until you all look new

but my shame is structural

& keeps on showing through.

Straight Shame

Two sides to a story; four to the drawer
which did for crib to a child born bang between
the Luftwaffe's last bomb and Sixties' swing
into the rationed metronome of Churchillian Britain.

First, the nan felt shame—her daughter just sixteen
and just the right side of wedlock when delivered
of her own daughter whose father was a stranger
until returned from country's service two years later.

Four decades on, skipping a generation, the shame
became the daughter's daughter's on seeing her son
would never be a man after her father's manner—
Brylcreemed and brawned, impregnating teenagers.

The same shame was son's inheritance until chosen
family raised him in his *other* ancestry—which mum
came to honour, in time. She also came to understand
a thing or two on the passing of her old nan—

that butter-wouldn't-melt woman burned inside so
she'd passed-off daughter's daughter as her own
and the child could never bond with birth-mum,
never felt smiled upon like later-born siblings.

No son of hers would feel for long similarly—
all are loved equally, though all have loved differently.

A Good Likeness

I have his eyes—fierce-fringed
as Stevie Nicks' tambourine—

another's brows arch over them—parabolic
as Eartha Kitt's delivery—

a third man gave me his lips—pursed tight
as Madonna Ciccone's career choreography—

a fourth gave me his voice—full-fruited
as Carmen Miranda's headdress—

a fifth gave his wrist—knowing
as Marilyn Monroe's hemline—

a sixth his hips—swishy
as Patricia Routledge's curtains—

none of these men were my father—
all are my mothers—birthing me

like Leigh Bowery—on dance floors
at rallies—and raising me

Bourne Rad

for Bette

When first we met you were wearing something butch
decorator's dungarees perhaps decoratively splashed
hair pineappled on top & right there in broad daylight
in the middle of a London street square-set in that
stubbled jawline Pantone 19-1764 TCX Lipstick Red

this boy from the backwater had never seen anything
like it before later I learnt to my cost that it could be
High Risk Red but most often it was just Jester Red
& always True Red borne on *your* terms like a wound
clawed from kittens upon whom you doted in dotage

voice purring not roaring BIG caterwauling as it had
on demonstrations in auditoriums gliding from glittering
East End to Quentin at the flip of a queen staking a flag
Radical Red in imaginations & in future generations
leaving your audience as you leave this world changed.

Prospects

for Derek

I first visited your garden
under library viewing station)
you became my obsession
I was encouraged to reach

on film (my hard on hidden
then in person (on art foundation)
(& subject of dissertation)
out (by kind tutor, Kathryn)

at this desk you wrote
me back in a script
as beautiful as it was
~~inscrutable~~
but I got the gist:
your body would not permit
our minds to meet

my jacket
is taken
as I step
through
the door
onto a floor
w h e r e

thankfully I found
your postcard, backside up
TOXO AIDS VICE BOYS
screaming in reproduction
into mother's doormat
visceral as impasto
outrages in your lounge

I imagine the photo of you
in the studio, in the shadow
of *Blue*, was captured
a few months later
at the film's premiere;
it was the only time
we were in the same room

decades
e a r l i e r
my hopeful
handwriting
lay waiting
T O B E
picked up

had I been older earlier
would we have known
each other; had I been
older earlier, would I still
be here at your bedside?
(linen bought for a fortune
at the same age I now am)

we're not meant
~~to go in~~
but the guide takes
a shine; *blue* pills
never lived
in your bathroom
as they do in my own

oh, to have worked with you

on your shelf, a book I worked on

we're told the kitchen is least *Jarman*;
on the table a book is open at a poem:
'I walk in this garden
holding the hands of dead friends
old age came quickly for my frosted generation
cold, cold, cold they died so silently'

my jacket is making
itself at home
in an extension
you never saw to completion;
I leave *my* writing
in your book (of visitation)
as you left yours in mine

you gave your garden
no boundary
but the horizon
so you sowed
we *all* are reaping

Pleasure Gardening
for the RVT

1662   The gratification of gossamer desire
was centuries-manured into her
Vauxhall plot: bridge & boat crowd
had flocked to find senses titillated
by restauranteurs, rope walkers
in revealing leg-wear transporting
them to stars & rent boys in rustling
arbours returning them to gutters.

1862   She scrunched her skirts & squatted
in a corner of what had once been
playground of kings (& queens);
there she remained—hem blackened
by road junction, brickwork ribbed
like crinoline & colour of piss stains
—a tavern royal only in name.

1962   The queens returned with servicemen
from frontlines. She welcomed them
—maintaining a merkin of legality
with hymen between stout-sipping
pensioners & female impersonators
synching & strutting a kidney-curve bar.

1987   Optics sightlined & stage centre-set
        for Savage put-downs, she fought
        bigot-gloved bobbies as she fought
        all viruses—capitalism especially—
        at each proud tit an underpuppy;
        she became Boudicca-upon-Thames.

2012   Well, what do we think she was doing,
        squatting in South London slum land?
        Shit is a nutrient; water-closet rude bits,
        wash out wildness & weird insects,
        you get Gail's growing in straight lines;
        this a good gardener overstands.

2024   Even warrior queens can fall, in the end;
        that Capital is a cunning one—milking
        the old girl for all she's got under cover
        of having her strapped to supporting
        machines—when all she needs, really
        is a sneaky ciggie, a swig of gin & to feel
        that filthy laugh rattling her doors again.

An Earthing

If, after a mouthful, Eve had let fall
the apple, retrieved it with Eden soil
sugared on bitten lips, my mother
would've had that in the rubbish,
knowledge only partially ingested

and heaven help us if any dirt
got traipsed into carpets, hotfooting
from the park at teatime to find
her sifting and folding air in, fighting
for a turn to tongue the spoon clean.

Earth should have a crumb structure
light as Mother's Victoria, its trick
of effortlessness the work of millions
of uncredited organisms for whom
loam is home—bugs best not supplanted

to human gut—she was probably right
about that: we are all mostly microbes,
inside us a universe fantastic as anything
captured by NASA, but an alien culture
can unbalance a delicate solar-system.

Mum flunked school-science but got
pH balance—mixing with gut-feeling
the correct cosmos of compost for any
salvaged shoot to root and flourish.

None of us grew as expected:
when my own florid form failed
to respond to pruning, she tried
repotting; I kept growing. Any fruit
conducts current, given grounding,
however far it may have fallen.

Battery Life

Like a reconditioned phone,
his body comes secondhand:
hardware from parents,
software from a childhood
of which he has select recollection.

Who can say if his cells were always
run-down completely, topped-up
fully to guarantee longevity;
he works with what he's given,
takes the charge where he can.

When the Spark is Gone

at storm's centre

there is no matter

in consummation

of a mutual desire

comes nullification

discharging its dark

lightning in lethal oxymorons

your positron met

my electron across

a crowded heaven

in union an undoing

between becoming

and going a nothing

Vacuum Bomb in the Living Room

one pushed a button

& the other found a sharp-tongued missile forming

falling four frames-per-second & scoring

one piñataed a petrol shimmer which entered unsealed egos

& the other sparked a paradox, its fire-filled snow-globe

exhausting oxygen, nulling lifeforms & ensuring nothing could grow again

Poetic Injustice

as green & gild
in a common field

Mammon & Mama Nature
might muck along together

an angel at each shoulder
but bending our ear

in only fortune's favour
nurtures a monoculture

that tosses the poor dead
in a separate bed

under potter's fields
but above the circle

of hell sodomites fill
according to Virgil

seen through the scales
of Dante's morals

Blood Sport

There was a Fox
in my class, his name after mine on the register;
we were often seated beside each other.

He was never a friend: there was something
of the runt about him—always yapping for attention,
his uniform with growth room, hair unfashioned.

Mine was brat-packed: I was desperate to fit, forget
my othering in junior playground, but schoolboys smelt
poof a mile off and hounded me, as they did Fox for *pikey*.

By third form, he'd grown into and out of that uniform—
still piss-streak thin but trousers mid-shin; they found him
suspended mid-air one morning.

We knew something was wrong when headmaster
interrupted our *here sir*s; an 'accident' had occurred:
I was now followed by Gomme on the register.

First lesson began, then; a second
takes years: we *pikeys* and *poofters*
are on the same team as each other.

A Chip off the Old Block

My report never read *he's good*
    with his hands:
I took home my name in hieroglyphs
    neatly-tapestried
& my sequined sphinxes were the envy
    of Year Three
but my mitts mutinied over
    any *masculinities*.

How I'd have loved to saw as well as sew
    straight, yet
my bird-box languished, lopsided
    on an outpost
past the greenhouse, safe from mocking
    male relatives.

My brother & father could do-it-yourself
    any shelf;
my grandfather could whisper furniture
    from stumps;
maybe that's why I was drawn, age eleven
    to the other
son of a carpenter who found himself
    born into wood
but would carve his own path with words
    water & fish.

Nathan the son of John, the husband
    of Glenda
the daughter of George, the builder
    I laboured under
underage in school holidays for pebbledash
    pocket money
wheeling a barrow wide of uncles who followed
    their father's trade
& lead in quips about my quiff & red top
    regurgitations:
that Marc Almond — seven pints of semen
    they sucked
from his gut! I tuned out to George Michael
    on a faithful radio
& then lost my religion to R.E.M
    two millennia
after Jesus lit upon his & left the family
    business; he was
nailed against grain for his pains.
    The end.

But if the beginning was the word & the word
    was God
that's staying power I can only hope for;
    our father
will not read anything into this poem
    or any other:
books are not for him, but he built the shelf
    mine stand upon.

41

Life Library

He finds it filed between *secateurs*
and *sewing-machine*, checks no one
is looking and selects *self-esteem*.

He's tempted to send it straight back
where it came from — shaped like an organ
or lebkuchen, he studies its sugared small-print.

Feel like a failure in all you do, that you never
'get the goal'? Can't bear to bare yourself
in the mirror anymore? Then this is for you!

The words refract and reflect through him,
promise a pot at the end of them. He thinks,
Let's see if it works then, circles the desk

a few times, feels his cheeks colouring
as the librarian scans it, saying, *You're lucky*
to find that in — one of our most popular items.

With the cynicism of a man who's never known
a world revolving around anything but pain,
he will resist transformation from third

to first person. For if my *but*s become *ands*,
if I don't want *and* I choose — who am I now?
And who, when loan is due, will I be tomorrow?

Great Depression

If they ask where I am, tell them: I am
wintering. I have secreted small acorns
of sadness in crevices of gnarled limbs
and shall be savouring their bitternesses
on the back of my tongue until the days
lengthen.

       But mainly, I'll be sleeping:
while they beaver away under skies
painted *Prussian Blue* and *Payne's Grey*,
I shall snore under layers of fat and fur
I worked for all year, until the days
wax warmer.

       Only then shall I venture
from my lair to take the spring air; sore
eyed, they'll stare, wonder *who is that
creature—so slender, so eager?* And
I'll declare *it is I, the grizzled bear* —
tendered make-over by *my* nature.

My Mass Extinctions

The first arrived as asteroid
across a playground—*Gaylord!*
so suddenly and with such velocity
there was no opportunity to shy
its trajectory; Tooth Fairies and Father
Christmases perished on impact:

I was it.

The second was volcanic
as a virgin dream, unconcealable
as pustules on teen skin;
the annihilation of generations
of convention came in hash clouds
and basalt-black combats:

I owned it.

The third rose as ocean
or audience, pattering like rain
for forty nights and forty days;
I soaked it up, took them in
in twos or threes or more—*Hurrah!*
my Noah was a hit:

I smashed it.

The fourth came in glaciation
of metre and rhyme, routine's *di-dum*,
contempt's comforting chime;
new form a challenge, I shovelled
gold, free-versed vertiginous
expectation:

I turned it around.

The fifth is hypoxia
of hope, slow failure
of ambition, the yearly grind
of inhibiting skeletons, flesh forsaking
bone like Sunday mutton, succumbing
to gravity:

I fight it, vainly.

The sixth may be manmade—
calculated as profits
from tapped veins, as overdosing
an ecosystem; *we are it*
and there is just one
way out of this:

own it, fight it, turn it around.

Medusa, Ma Sœur

I sloughed my straight skin
—a risqué routine
among the humdrum mis-en-scene
of my mother's kitchen;

my sister didn't blink
—eyes lidless as a python
& arms constrictor-firm
but words in my ear, warm.

There was no blood between us
—only XY chromosomes
would grow in Mother's womb;
at home, I had no one

with whom to play 'hair'
—all through Infants & Juniors
I'd been searching
in Hannahs & Claires

for my missing sibling.
I found her in Seniors, in a Sarah
—permed & perfect, so
superior to our peers; a piper

I followed her, Eros-eyed
—in corridors, in orchestras
but our love was no food
for which we'd been prepared

(with apologies, Whitney—
the *greatest* is not of *yourself*
but between cis-sis
& fag-frère).

I have lost her, found her
—iron-haired, older
shorter & taller—
grown as serpent-teeth sown

across time zones
into a legion of warrior-queens
for whom there is no stone
I would ever leave unturned.

Summertime, Sleepless

floundering

as a fish

sea's blanket

stripped from it

naked as earth

on a cloudless night

reading our moon

on the needle

of a building

I see ships

passing

Ovid, Interrupted

Waist-deep, you beckon
　　　　but I'm frozen
　　you are warm-welling
　　　　I, unthawing

Like Narcissus, I reflect
　　　　upon this stasis
　　unlike him, I find
　　　　myself unchanging

So before my frost bites
　　　　skin, Echo swim
　　until your love meets
　　　　its mirroring

Narcissus Knocks Up a Salad

With the joy of a sharp knife
through the tomato's denial,
I'll tell you I'm leaving. In truth,
I've not been here for some time—
my absence noted as your smiles
dined unaccompanied and your eyes
mirrored morsels my strict heart
metered to our bowl. You'll cry and ply
me with future tenses. I shall remain
self-righteously stone-eared, slam doors
to cupboards—*where have you put*
the salt and pepper—call you
for dinner.

A Palatable Untruth

Make me a monster:
baste me in your sourest flavours;

garnish me with hooves, horns;
hell, give me breath that burns

good grief from our bones, for an astringent
finish will better complement

this rehash. Serve well
chilled until all former mutuals

take it to be true—
only someone evil could no longer need you.

Broken

I have wanted to remain
firm and white
with yolk untouched

centre-plate
but how comforting
to curl within:

the whole world
yellow as a pastel
de nata I bought

for your breakfast
when our Lisbon expedition
was abandoned in Autumn;

yellow as a daisy
floret on your favourite
Winter knitwear.

Spring, now
you're not here;
yellow everywhere.

Cookies

anxious about arrangements or even
separation, you spent our last evening
displacing flour & sugar, oil & water
into earthenware, bringing them
together with a pinch of *je ne sais quoi*
& baking a quarter-hour   it's twenty-four
since you were here; my souvenirs
sit in Tupperware, sweetly uncomplex
& quite unlike your mixed tapas
of aegean saltiness, amaro bitterness
& umami deep-dish   I am left
with a sourness, two words & one image
you've not read my message
& you're not wrong to turn down
our oven: no two batches can be
the same; a mistake I made
with the last kookie man, sun-licked
one autumn & seconded in spring
with frosting, but then & then
your chips in my head, crumb trails
in my bed

The Knowledge

is within us   a cartography
of queerness   unfolded
on *Smalltown* platforms
contours clear as bloodlines
as hunting calls on playgrounds
known as backs of hands
rote as routes   out of boyhood
gridlock   razored as retorts
on the portcullis of campness
curlicued as the consonants
of primetime palatalisation
salted as wounds   from legacy
legislation   sweet as ass
holy as matrimony

The Slow-Burn of the Long-Term Relationship

It's the same every weekend—
drawing straws for chores,
cleaning and cooking then
hearing that story an *nth* time at dinner.

You'll desert dishes till morning, knowing
I'll wash them before you awaken—
it's the same every weekend.
But then, again we're rolling

and sparking, plumes rising—
it's the same every weekend.
The Beast with Two Wings
rides our rainbow to its end

then dies on bedlinen, is ashen
in my toothbrushing, cold as your
feet or fridge-foraged leftover—
it's the same every weekend.

Man Shed

don't take it personally, dear
if I glaze over
like a lake in winter
my coolness may seem clear
but crystal water is never as it appears
shift happens down there
at rock-bottom temperatures
& if my glacial backatchas
drive your temper ever higher
our ecosystems will fall out of kilter
for I cannot be summer all year
my mind's microbes need winter
to confer in secret strata
so if I take myself to our perimeter
or earth's end for an hour
please don't take it personally, my dear

Mon Cher

I'd never have looked twice
in town; in Arcadia, I saw
hidden spectrums, heard
your siren song, swam
into your sun & berthed
salt-buoyant in your arms.

I got you, you said & played
Cher in bed on the morning
you left; *You Better Sit Down
Kids* just shuffled on & there
was I thinking I was fine:
one wave & I'm gone.

Lost Property

Yes, I have baggage—you gif
with camp counterpoint to the serious
seam we seem to be threading; I ping
back an emoticon that can't decide
if it's laughing or crying—*don't we all, hun.*

Until now, we've offered ourselves only
fetish-fleshed and, seductively shiny,
have rebuffed all scrutiny. I feel flattered
you feel able to unzip a little, reveal
the wound we all gaily carry.

Pink and perfumed as an orifice,
I'm disgusted/delighted as you proceed
to pull soiled smalls from it: Ta-Dah!
Trauma! Disorder! Dependence
on drug-divined euphoria!

My own fissure has been long-sutured
by a miscellany of therapies, weeps only
modestly/manfully; yours is still
seeping through a recent addressing.
I nightingale a hard-won song—

some like to dance around hand-luggage,
I prefer to unpack it. You smile,
in simulacrum; our thread darts
through gym routines and other less
weighty material then, on the hem

of our next hook-up, is abruptly cut.
Receiving no reciprocation—not even
a tick of acknowledgement—I apprehend
a deep thrum, the transmission
of pain, as though you are in me again

and circling the case you left, closed
in my head, I trace an arc between
markers of the places you've been
(from abandonment to rehabilitation)
and mourn my misplaced projection

in which you allow yourself to be
unlocked—soft-furnishings
spilling/spreading; lungs for lampshades,
guts for garlands—and make of me
your home.

A Tale of Two Metronomes

We clicked when we met;
our beats synced sweetly
but were actually set
to subtly varied tempi—

Bowie vocal doubling
becoming a clattering
Ligeti symphonic poem
or sprockets in old film

looping your trauma
and projecting perpetrators
onto my features
as in Bergman's *Persona*

or as old couples grow similar;
could we have sung through
our discordant Act Two
to curtain in rhythm once more?

Desert Island Dreams

Thank you, Sue-slash-Kirsty-slash-Lauren
for that hyperbolic/hypothetic introduction.
My first song was conceived the same year as me,
though I didn't listen to it until touching twenty.
I mean, I must have heard it before then
—in the car, on the radio in the kitchen—
but he was just some shot-star Dad didn't care for
whose back-catalogue was still in my future.

Rebel Rebel (Bowie)

My childhood was happily unhungry: I hadn't yet
appetite for what I didn't know I lacked. This next
track was playing on the doorstep of adolescent
awakening. I was just out of junior school, resplendent
in eighties pastel; Mum was dancing, a beaded queen
—which in my woollen-eyes, she always had been—
but I was mortified in the clubhouse on the campsite
as she was crowned for her moves that summer night.

Into the Groove (Madonna)

Lying unsleeping, age eleven, I remember divining
that God must be fiction. Then a crusader masquerading
as teacher colonised my mind at the Grammar
and administered Jesus as a sticking plaster
over a sexuality I'd yet to discover. I could've chosen
something from a Passion, but this I performed when
seventeen and have loved ever since: it has the beauty,
the spirituality, but not the bloody Christianity.

Concerto for Oboe & Violin, 2nd movement (Bach)

Any last vestige of holiness dissipated at art college,
where I met my first love. Though I didn't manage
to bed him, he did bed in the foundation of my
tape collection: musical miles I couldn't afford to buy
were borrowed, copied, committed to memory.
Patti, PJ, Morrissey… It has to be something early
before he became such a *boor*, and this sums up for me
that year before university, aching to be free.

How Soon Is Now? (The Smiths)

I lost my virginity in an Oxford dormitory to an old
Etonian who became my first boyfriend. The manifold
distance between me and my family grew exponentially
as he taught me to *speak properly*, what to see
—including my first opera production. I've chosen
this section as I can imagine listening to its evocation
of moonlight as I sit on my beach at night, reflecting
on reflections, waxing and waving.

Third Sea Interlude from Peter Grimes (Britten)

By the time I got to London, I'd already begun to see
someone who had a place in town. He winded me
beneath his wing a few years as I got shit together,
then took off with a Karen Carpenter impersonator.
Here's the original, on solitude—which I've made
peace with: I was single for the next decade,
more or less, and came in time to understand
a man with no man is not necessarily an island.

Solitaire (The Carpenters)

Work became my primary relationship and boys—
of whom there were many—but background noise.
Most were overnight sensations; some hung
around for a few messages, meets, months.
My last long-term long-sighted me when I was
strutting my stuff in a remix of *The Wizard of Oz*
for an age of identity politics—a creative high-noon
which, of course, included a rendition of this tune.

Over the Rainbow (Judy Garland)

We were *à deux* longer than I was ever
alone and still—like ABBA—make work together:
familiarity can heighten creative conception
and contraction. Perhaps we didn't dance as often
as he might have liked: it isn't my *kind of thing.*
I wouldn't normally do this, as Pet Shop Boys sing,
but when I'm cast away and no one is looking, I'll whisk
all my clothes off and prance about to this.

Rite of Spring (Stravinsky)

If I had to save just one disc from the sea it would be
that last. Bible and Shakespeare I know you'll give me:
the former will make useful touch-paper; the latter
I'll use to entertain animals in a one-man extravaganza.
For my luxury—my oboe, please, and an endless supply
of reeds. That's incidental music sorted. And for my
book, Proust: finally, I'll have time to remember.
Thank you, Sue/Kirsty/Lauren: it's been a pleasure.

On the Privatisation of Pleasure

1.
Make mine an American-accented
exuberance of champagne & fruit
in a flute, not the British Bucks Fizz
of flat festive brunches & aunties
at parties, losing *inhibitions* & taking
nephews *from behind* à la Eurovision.

2.
Mimosa, harbinger of spring
in February gloom, golden
shower of bloom, brazen
as a rubber queen's trim
promising torrential passion
in the privacy of the bathroom.

3.
Piss to Ass Plug, £61.99, Water
Sports Socks, £16.99, Ultra Urinal
Gag, £249, Rubber Surf Suit
with Contrast Colour, £429,
shipping, free on orders over £50,
dispatched in discreet packaging.

4.

Last year, I purloined pompom fronds
from a neighbour's garden at dawn,
surreptitiously snipping escapees
from private property, vaulting
fencing to feel the fresh air
of a public thoroughfare.

5.

The yellow arpeggios on my piano
sustained a day or two in their glass
vial; on the street, a floral free-for-all
until well into April, fading finally
in deep orange orgies: this year,
I sipped straight from the tree.

Circadian Cicadas

Males gather in woodland
for copulation, play their bodies
like car alarms each dawn.

*Keep it down! Some of us
are still sleeping!* I mean, who is that
racket meant to attract?

Obviously, they're not getting any:
all day, in and out of sequence
like some Steve Reich composition

until dusk conducts a silence,
welcome as liberation from testosterone
to an aging cruising-queen.

Laser-Like

he comes at sundown
  to sit at my feet
I know what he wants
  & make him wait

he knows I want it
  as much as him
& given time
  needs must give in

my love is directional
  & only revealed
on meeting resistance
  from another's particles

in-bush insecure
  never bird in paw
& yet he could chase
  its trail for hours

until our game
  begins to bore him
& he withdraws
  into gloaming's wanting

Mercury Rising

for Freddie

Did they hunt as we do
through room after room hungry
for you? Did Delilah brush Dalis
dislodge Lalique vases? Did Dorothy scale
keys in wrong-pawed rhapsodies?
Did Tom tear upholstery top to bottom
like temple curtain *abandoned again*
& who can rescue him this time?

Mary, Mary, clean & squeaky
in the movie? If only you'd loved her only
& not those boys with their moustaches
& diseases. Mary who got almost everything
which she is now getting rich from selling
including a moustache-comb by Tiffany
namesake to another pussy.

Did she preen her whiskers on its prongs
when you were gone perfume pulse points
with *odeur de maître*? Did you endure
in gussets of the catsuits sniffed by Oscar
& manequined three decades later
beneath a kimono murmuration
defying the laws of gravity at auction?
Now, I could see myself in one of *them*.

You were too *too* for me
back then. With no question
concerning his own orientation
Dad could admire without complication
your show-manliness on television sets
your vocal-prowess on *Greatest Hits*
cassettes. My head transduced nothing
but magnetic repulsion.

Had you lived longer or I Londoned sooner
& our streams crossed at the trough
of some black-eyed bar we'd have traded
catty quips leather-care tips I like to think
Miko claimed for collar a letter-studded
number cuff or cock-ring I wonder
how the trail of tourists translate this *P.I.G*
penned between kitty-piccies & ashtrays.

Were my lot happier I could bid
on *this* lot gilt-rim my butts extra
my ordinary that's all we're all seeking
surely & maybe it's what Dad found
in you & fostered in me? For him, then
going not gone should I go for a song
sketched on airline stationery but *burning
through the sky* indelibly, unstoppably.

Genet, A Cat Called

You, too, were an orphan, entrusted
to our care. You'd been called

Tigger by former carers: you were ginger,
stripy and had a bounce about you, sure

but we could only live with something queer.
It was a name you grew into as — *Prisoner*

not *of Love* but a one-bed in Dalston,
no *Balcony* even — you stole our affection,

high-wired our irritation with vespertine
dare-devilling and alarm-call caterwauling.

Your fall was sudden, your wound well-hidden;
we petitioned a veterinarian

for your life, a *Miracle* overnight
but by morning were planning *Funeral Rites*

with a cremator from Sunnyfields who struggled
with your Frenchified syllables.

Would your namesake have staked his place
between us, as you did, or else

pawed at the bedroom door, marked our bodies
possessively, memories, indelibly?

Avian Autopsy

We were never exactly of a plume:
you were into nesting; I was more free
as a—Zephyr-surfing, mountain-Musing
—that sort of thing. You would lay

eggs for me to sit on; I could never
be arsed: I'd crack one open, separate
origin from albumen and churn
artisan iced-dream. If you had wings,

you wouldn't use them; I made strap-ons
but word about Icarus had flown
around: harnessed and fetish-feathered,
you were scared to leave

the ground. Maybe you're more
mammalian: I hope you find an otter
or weasel to bring home wattle and daub
it with blessings; I'm off chasing Cherubim.

Leap Of/f

I am a boy who's discovered
he is also a bird and I'm perched
on a branch outside my window
enjoying a new view of the palace
I live in when I spy my brother
through a window on an upper floor
tied to a chair as our father clippers
the wings I didn't know my sibling
had grown and find my own
ruffled by feelings which frighten me
more than flying my home
so I falter from tree to tree
until I'm deep beneath their canopy
but my father's familiar is sent
to return me to princely captivity
and although this seems exciting
for some reason I also know I could
not accept any man's dominion now
I've felt flight's freedom so I keep on
flapping but mature wings beat faster
than a fledging's and the familiar's path
above treetops is unobstructed
whereas I must dodge trunks
and twigs in which my feathers
get twisted as I run the scene over
and again to refine the plotting
to maintain the tension between wanting
liberation and needing subjugation
but it's a difficult balance so I find
myself falling in a clearing and hearing
something swooping and

                        only on waking
do I become aware I must be captured
if my story is to move forward
for only as I fight to be free will
the familiar declare she is my mother
who was ensnared by my father
to whom she bore me and my brother
though my father forbade her to reveal
herself because he was ashamed
of his desires but my nature
must be honoured as both man
and avian and she's pursued me
only to offer her blessing to go
on flying into my binary birth-right
despite this meaning I may be hunted
in bird-form and she shan't see me
again and
                        the more I wake the more
I lose her and the more questions
I need answered about why she suffered
so long in gilded confinement
but then I recall my shaven sibling
and realise he is the reason she stays
with the king and goes on singing
her tame song but
                        now I'm awake
fully I still feel the wild call within me
which will tear out my throat unless
I release it and
                        birds outside have woken
so I go to my window to listen but
                                        it's still
dark so I can only sense the forest beyond
the ledge beneath my clawed feet and

The Things You Do

'I put a spell on you
Because you're mine'
Screamin' Jay Hawkins

time	to
cast	your
spell	again
darling	time
to	reach
in	and
cast	your
spell	again
I'm	starting
to	come
round	see
splotches	on
your	skin
so	open
mine	reach
in	and
cast	your
spell	again

74

Sleeve Notes

for George

MAKE IT BIG was my first album / *Happy Xmas love Nan* / poster slipped between vinyl & cover / two gentlemen chilling in smart casuals / not tacky at all / tacked to bedroom wall / until it fell apart at foldout seams // it seemed to take forever to grow my hair / it was almost as voluminous as yours by yuletide next year / Aunty asked me to DJ her party / my decks double cassette player / EVERYTHING SHE WANTS was floor-filler / cousin Donna seemed undeterred by its casual misogyny as she led the charge // your charges / in the nineties / shone a beam on your aversion to women / lewd acts with men had been denied robustly / in the eighties / by aunties across the country / *George Michael? Don't think so!* / my own wrinkled her nose / as at BO // body odour was something you seemed to be savouring / when I found FAITH / at the record store / only later did I discover armpits & assholes / could be filthy in a good way / *When you think what they do! It's disgusting!* / Mum scowled across the bows of my burgeonings / were your brazenings lubrication to reconciliation? / your voice does things to Mum / never done by any other man / lost or living // in the living-room LAST CHRISTMAS was playing / my boyfriend & his mother sobbing / news had come in / when Wham! bit dust it was just a matter of time before you asked me to form a new twosome / we would wear white shorts / when we almost-met we were wearing black suits / you sang SECRET LOVE

His Master's Voice

Some bequeathed breakfast habits—
toast with tomatoes and Marmite,
a lemon-water Master-reset.

One left him smooth as an egg
from brow to butt, the itch exquisite
agony for days; perversion remained

razor-written on his expression
until regrowth wiped it clean again.
Mum wasn't impressed but minded

the shackle at clavicle less; if only
she knew its only key was held by a Daddy
who knew its weight would release

the wait from shoulders squaring
to their beta nature. Another marked
his mettle with steel through each nipple—

visible in relief beneath smart-casuals—
and sealed their nuptials with a ring
which startled casual-bystanders

at the office urinal. A good Sir inscribed
him, first in vermillion signatures
which did not endure, then indigo curlicues

spelling his destiny, indelibly, upon his body.
But he didn't begin to become the void
he was meant to be until slipped inside

a hole-black skin and left reflecting
in the corner of a solar-system
as Master got on with celestial things;

only on attainment of an objectivity
Buddha would've envied, did Master see
fit to address him in hypnotic tones:

Slave swallowed each suggestion, seeking
completion—as so many men before him—
in submission to the will of a greater being.

The Maestro

with pitch-perfect irony, on attaining
mastery of his own body & the bodies
of those men who worship with him

on finally fine-tuning every nuance
of melody, harmony, tempo, rhythm
to orchestrate major symphonies

from minor vulnerabilities, in control
sufficiently to surrender self completely
& conduct this *them* to mutual ovation

his baton begins wavering with humdrum
imprecisions, his ear humming dissonance
in magnetic resonance imagings

repeated as the invasion of medical
instrumentation & metric as the counting
of tablets; his gowns are now hospital ones

I Hear a Queerphony

On first entry, he is shaky;
he has practised repeatedly
but the body betrays when accompanied
and the mind is a chorus of criticism
over which he cannot hear
the key changing: on second entry,
he plays a note wrongly;
the choir crescendo to derision:
on third, he solos *sempre forte*
in compensation; *listen to me, listen
and forget those other instruments!*

Knee-tapped with faint acclaim
by players around him, he widens
his spotlight to include them:
on fourth entry, he duets tunefully
with a neighbour; on fifth, he ventures
so far as to follow the leader; sixth,
the conductor; seventh, audience.

He learns to listen to their expressions;
he learns to listen to reverberations
of queerstory: beneath the roguery
of Tchaikovsky's waltz in five,
the agony of being forbidden
to dance with a man you love.

By last entry, he will have left the building,
but with the understanding, like those
before him, that something of themselves
remains within—some progression
beyond the lifecycle of applause
and acclaim—*listen to them, listen.*

A Gaylord's Prayer

Uncultured pearls, my rosary—
You Ancestors, cum unto me!
You Unicorns, Fauns & Centaurs,
Codebreakers & Lawmakers!

Hail Marys, Nellies & Nancies,
Narcissuses & Pansies!
Hail Gaol-House Balladeers,
Duckies & Darlings & Dears!

Praise to Punks & Gender-Benders!
Praise to the Bloomsbury-Setters,
Cross-Dressers, Shirt-Lifters,
Shit-Stabbers, Soldiers, Sailors!

Blessed be the Gavestons,
Ganymedes & the Jarmans!
Blessed Starmen, Superstellar
Forever Famous Factoryworkers!

Glory be to Whoopsies, Witches!
Glory be to the Daddies
& to the Boys & the Two-Spirits!
Glories to Fairies & Flamers & Faggots!

Our day is dark; You defied darker—
Vanguardian Angels! Light Forebearers!
Disciples & Divine Drag Queens,
Sodomites & Sebastians!

We are Scions to Your Stock!
With your Leaven, we rise up!
You are Molly; we are Spoon—
Fantabulosa Fruit of Your Womb!

As it was for all eternity
is now & ever shall be—
our world without end.
Gaymen.

Notes

p17 In the gay slang Polari, bold means daring/homosexual.

p18 Trash Palace was a gay venue in Soho (2000s); Substation South was a gay venue in Brixton (1990s-2000s); Ghetto was a gay venue in Soho (2001-8); blue light is emitted by the mobile phones used to access hook-up apps.

p19 Blitz was an inclusive club-night in Covent Garden (1979-80); Caravan Club was a gay-friendly club in Covent Garden (1934); Dionysius was the Greek god of bacchanalian excesses (including pansexuality); Apollo was the Greek god of poetry (whose male lovers included Hyacinthus); Marvellous was a gay club-night in Brixton (1990s-2000s); Mother Bar was a venue in Hoxton (1990s-2000s), hosting gay nights; Misfits was a gay club-night in Soho, (2000s); gay men are sometimes called friends of Dorothy—who, in the 1939 film *The Wizard of Oz*, gets home by clicking her heels together three times.

p21 'Don't Die of Ignorance' was a 1980s public health information campaign about AIDS, featuring tombstones.

p22 In the USA, queer cooperatives have been renting land to run community farms; Pre-Exposure Prophylaxis (PrEP) reduces the risk of HIV transmission during sex.

p23 In dominant/submissive sexual relationships, the dom may be referred to as Sir.

p24 In dominant/submissive sexual relationships, the sub may be referred to as boy; many fetishists are into sex in gear, such as leather; twinks are gay men of youthful appearance; polyamorists have multiple concurrent relationships; jocks are gay men of athletic build; monogamists have relationships with only one person at a time; otters are lean and hairy; geeks may be introverts and gamers; pups are into canine roleplay; daddies are older men who have relationships with younger ones; bears are big and hairy; cubs are young bears; a chaser is someone of one type who fetishizes those of another type, for instance, slim men who chase larger ones; pigs are into bodily odours and excesses; queers tend to have fluid gender identities and sexualities; discreet men keep their sexuality secret; trans humans have a gender identity which is not the same as the sex assigned to them at birth.

p25 The rainbow flag uses the colours of the spectrum to represent the diversity of the LGBTQ+ community

p27 Rainbow-washing is when companies use LGBTQ+ imagery without genuinely supporting the LGBTQ+ community.

p29 Madonna (1958-) has been a prominent and consistent advocate for LGBTQ+ rights; queer performance artist Leigh Bowery (1961-1994) 'gave birth' to wife Nicola at Kinky Gerlinky nightclub.

p30 Bette Bourne was a queer actor and activist (1939-2024).

p31 Follows the ground plan of Prospect Cottage, home of queer filmmaker and artist, Derek Jarman (1942-1994).

p32 Royal Vauxhall Tavern (1862-) is an LGBTQ+ venue.

p38 Dante (1265-1321) placed sodomites in the seventh circle of hell in his poem *Inferno*.

p41 Marc Almond is a queer singer-songwriter (1957-); R.E.M. were fronted by queer singer-songwriter Michael Stipe (1960-)

p49 In *Metamorphoses*, Ovid (43BC-18AD) recounts the story of Narcissus—who falls in love with his own image and is transformed into a flower—and Echo—who falls in love with him and is reduced to her voice alone.

p54 'Smalltown Boy' is a 1984 song by gay group Bronski Beat; Section 28 prohibited local authorities from 'promoting homosexuality' between 1988 and 2003.

p59 Chemsex is the use of drugs (specifically Meth, Meph and GHB) to enhance sex; it is most common among gay men.

p62 Morrissey (1959-) is a bisexual singer-songwriter and former frontman of The Smiths; Benjamin Britten (1913-76) was a composer and conductor who lived openly with his lover, tenor Peter Pears (1910-1986).

p64 Yellow symbolises urine on the fetish scene.

p66 Cruising is the pursuit of sex in public spaces, like parks.

p68 Delilah, Dorothy, Tom, Tiffany, Oscar and Miko were cats belonging to Freddie Mercury (1946-91), frontman of Queen, whose other belongings—when he died of AIDS—were left to Mary Austin, who auctioned them at Sotheby's in 2023. Songs include 'Don't Stop Me Now'.

p70 *Prisoner of Love, The Balcony, Miracle of the Rose* and *Funeral Rights* are by gay novelist and playwright Jean Genet (1910-1986), namesake of Inkandescent's beloved feline intern (2015-22).

p74 Fisting is a sexual activity where a hand is inserted into the rectum.

p75 *Make It Big* is an album by Wham! including 'Everything She Wants'; 'Secret Love' appears on *Songs from the Last Century* which, along with *Faith*, is an album by singer-songwriter George Michael (1963-2016), who came out in 1998, following his arrest for 'public lewdness'.

p77 Master/Slave is a consensual sexual relationship structure in which one individual serves another.

p79 The *Sixth Symphony* by Pyotr Ilyich Tchaikovsky (1840-1893) was premiered nine days before the composer died, possibly by suicide due to depression as a result of his homosexuality.

p80 Fauns and centaurs were sexually omnivorous mythological creatures; Alan Turing (1912-1954) was a codebreaker during World War II who committed suicide following his chemical castration after prosecution for homosexual acts; Lord Arran (1910-1983) was the lawmaker who pushed for the decriminalisation of homosexuality in the Sexual Offences Act 1967, following the suicide of his gay brother; mary, nelly, nancy, pansy, whoopsie, fairy, flamer, faggot, punk, shirt-lifter and shit-stabber have all been used to refer to gay men; witches have long been associated with alternative sexualities; darling and dear have often been used by gay men to address each other; Oscar Wilde (1854-1900) was convicted of gross indecency with other males and sentenced to two years hard labour, during which he wrote *The Ballad of Reading Gaol*; Duckie are LGBTQ+ club runners; gender-bender was used in the 1980s to describe artists such as Boy George (1961-); the Bloomsbury Group were artists and writers known for their liberated sexuality, including Virginia Woolf (1882-1941), John Maynard Keynes (1883-1946), E.M Forster (1879-1970), and Duncan Grant (1885-1978); cross-dressers wear clothes traditionally associated with the opposite gender; homosexuality was standard-practice amongst Spartan soldiers in Ancient Greece; Moby Dick by Hermann Melville features a marriage between two sailors; Piers Gaveston (1284-1312) was the lover of Edward II (1284-1327), as portrayed in the play of that name by Christopher Marlowe (1564-1593); Ganymede was a youth abducted by the god Zeus to be his 'cupbearer'; during a performance of his single 'Starman' on *Top of the Pops*, David Bowie (1947-2016) put an arm around guitarist Mick Ronson in homoerotic fashion; gay artist Andy Warhol (1928-1987) supposedly said, 'In the future, everyone will be famous for fifteen minutes' and superstars at his studio, The Factory, included Candy Darling (1944-74); two-spirits is used by Indigenous North Americans to describe those with male and female characteristics; it is rumoured that Jesus had a relationship with disciple, John; Divine (1945-88) was an actor and singer best known for work with John Waters (1946-); Saint Sebastian is subject of many homoerotic artworks; Molly Houses were meeting places for homosexual men in eighteenth century Britain where mock births involving wooden dolls, or spoons were staged; in Polari, fantabulosa means fabulous and fruit means queen.

Acknowledgements

Thank you to publisher Justin David for his encouragement.

To editor Joelle Taylor for her insight and inspiration.

And to designer Michael Long for his fantabulosa cover.

To Ellen McAteer for proofreading, along with her fellow Kings Poets—Catherine McLoughlin, Jess Grynfeld, Rita Suszek, Ernesto Sarezale and Olive Franklin—whose fire helped forge every poem.

And to the publications who put beta versions in print: *Magma*, who published 'Blitz Club & Caravan', 2025; Muswell Press, who published 'Old Queen as Ecosystem' in *Queer Life, Queer Love 2*, 2023; the Royal Society of Literature, who published 'Bulbs' in *Write Across London*, 2020; *Poetry Wales*, who published 'A Good Likeness', 'Bourne Rad' and 'Medusa, Ma Sœur', 2026; *Seaford Review*, who published 'Pleasure Gardening', 2025; *The Broken Spine*, who published 'A Chip Off the Old Block', 2025; *Ink, Sweat & Tears*, who published 'Great Depression', 2025; *Impossible Archetype,* who published 'Narcissus Knocks Up a Salad', 2021; *Fourteen Poems*, who published 'Broken', 2023; *Stepaway Magazine*, who published 'The Knowledge', 2025; Broken Sleep, who published 'Lost Property' in *Masculinity: An Anthology of Modern Voices*, 2024; *Atelier International*, who published 'On the Privatisation of Pleasure', 2025; *Queerlings*, who published 'Avian Autopsy', 2022.

To the Keith Collins Will Trust for their kind permission to reproduce the quote from *Modern Nature* by Derek Jarman, copyright © Derek Jarman, 1991.

And to Lynn and Nick who gave me 'time and place' to finish this book, fittingly, at The Prospect.

Also from Inkandescent

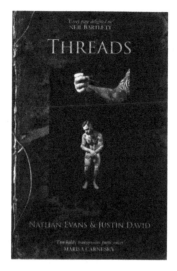

THREADS
by Nathan Evans & Justin David

If Alice landed in London not Wonderland this book might be the result. Threads is the first collection from Nathan Evans, each poem complemented by a bespoke photograph from Justin David and, like Tenniel's illustrations for Carroll, picture and word weft and warp to create an alchemic (rabbit) whole.

On one page, the image of an alien costume, hanging surreally beside a school uniform on a washing line, accompanies a poem about fleeing suburbia. On another, a poem about seeking asylum accompanies the image of another displaced alien on an urban train. Spun from heartfelt emotion and embroidered with humour, Threads will leave you aching with longing and laughter.

'In this bright and beautiful collaboration, poetry and photography join hands, creating sharp new ways to picture our lives and loves.'
NEIL BARTLETT

'Two boldly transgressive poetic voices'
MARISA CARNESKY

Also from Inkandescent

by Nathan Evans

'Poignant, humane and uncompromising'
STEPHEN MORRISON-BURKE

As King Cnut proved, tide and time wait for no man:
An AnthropoScene, the first part of this collection, dives into the rising tides of geo-political change, the second, Our Future Is Now Downloading, explores sea-changes of more personal natures.

Nathan's debut, Threads, was longlisted for the Polari First Book Prize. His follow-up bears all the watermarks of someone who's swum life's emotional spectrum. Short and (bitter)sweet, this is poetry for a mobile generation, poetry for sharing – often humorous, always honest about contemporary human experience, saying more in a few lines than politicians say in volumes, it offers an antidote to modern living.

'a kaleidoscopic journey brimming with vivid imagery, playfulness and warmth—a truly powerful work'
KEITH JARRETT

nkandescent

Inkandescent Publishing was established in 2016
by Justin David and Nathan Evans to shine a light on
diverse and distinctive voices.

Could you do one Inkredible thing for us?
Sign up to our mailing list so we can keep you informed
about future releases:

www.inkandescent.co.uk/sign-up

follow us on **Facebook**:
@InkandescentPublishing

on **Twitter/X**:
@InkandesentUK

on **Instagram**:
@inkandescentuk

on **BlueSky**:
@inkandescentuk.bsky.social

and on **Threads**:
@inkandescentuk